Dear Molly, Dear Olive

Molly Gets a Goat
(and Wants to Give It Back)

written by
Megan Atwood

illustrated by
Gareth Llewhellin
and Lucy Fleming

PROPERTY OF
TTLE PUBLIC LIBRARY

PICTURE WINDOW BOOKS
a capstone imprint

Dear Molly, Dear Olive is published by Picture Window Books,
a Capstone Imprint
1710 Roe Crest Drive
North Mankato, Minnesota 56003
www.mycapstone.com

Copyright © 2019 Picture Window Books

All rights reserved. No part of this publication may be reproduced in whole or in part, or stored in a retrieval system, or transmitted in any form or by any means, electronic, mechanical, photocopying, recording, or otherwise, without written permission of the publisher.

Library of Congress Cataloging-in-Publication Data
Names: Atwood, Megan, author. | Llewhellin, Gareth, illustrator. | Fleming, Lucy, illustrator.
Title: Molly gets a goat (and wants to give it back) / by Megan Atwood ;
illustrated by Gareth Llewhellin and Lucy Fleming.
Description: North Mankato, Minnesota : Picture Window Books, [2018] | Series: Dear Molly, Dear Olive |
Summary: Molly, who lives in New York City, and Olive, who lives on a farm in Iowa, are email friends, and both think that the other would be in serious trouble if they exchanged places—so they make a bet, and while Olive is getting totally lost in Minneapolis, Molly is at a farm in upstate New York desperately trying to fend off a goat.
Identifiers: LCCN 2018009425 (print) | LCCN 2018010379 (ebook) |
ISBN 9781515829232 (eBook PDF) | ISBN 9781515829218 (library binding) |
ISBN 9781684360406 (paperback)
Subjects: LCSH: Farm life—Juvenile fiction. | City and town life—Juvenile fiction. |
Best friends—Juvenile fiction. | Pen pals--Juvenile fiction. | Letter writing—Juvenile fiction. |
Humorous stories. | New York (State)--Juvenile fiction. | Minneapolis (Minn.)—Juvenile fiction. |
CYAC: Farm life--Fiction. | City and town life--Fiction. | Best friends—Fiction. | Friendship—Fiction. |
Pen pals--Fiction. | Letter writing—Fiction. | Humorous stories. | New York (State)—Fiction. |
Minneapolis (Minn.)—Fiction. | LCGFT: Humorous fiction.Classification: LCC PZ7.A8952 (ebook) |
LCC PZ7.A8952 Mp 2018 (print) |
DDC 813.6 [Fic] —dc23
LC record available at https://lccn.loc.gov/2018009425

Editor: Gina Kammer
Designers: Aruna Rangarajan and Tracy McCabe
Production Specialist: Kris Wilfahrt

Design Elements: Shutterstock

Printed in Canada.
PA020

Table of Contents

Dear Molly,
Dear Olive

Molly and Olive are best friends — best friends who've never met! Two years ago, in second grade, they signed up for a cross-country Pen Pal Club. Their friendship was instant.

Molly and Olive send each other letters and email. They send postcards, notes, and little gifts too. Molly lives in New York City with her mom and younger brother. Olive lives on a farm near Sergeant Bluff, Iowa, with her parents. The girls' lives are very different from one another. But Molly and Olive understand each other better than anyone.

Chapter 1

Molly in the Country

Molly

Dear Olive,

How are you? Mom thought it was time I wrote a real letter instead of an email to you. So here it is! I'm so excited for this weekend. Damien and I get to visit Aunt Gen by ourselves in Poughkeepsie, New York! She's so much fun. Plus, I'll get to see what it's like in the country, like where you live! Aunt Gen says Poughkeepsie isn't the "country" — it's a city. But my mom says it might as well be the country compared to New York. I can't wait to play in big fields and make friends with mice or something. Isn't that what people

7

do in the country? Just a big old break from having to DO things all the time would be great. I bet that's what it's like for you all the time! You're so lucky.

I'll let you know how it goes!

Best friends forever,

Molly

~ Molly ~

Two days seemed like a loooonng time to wait, but that was how long my letters took getting to Olive. It took all of my willpower not to just email her.

I was so excited to go to the country again. After I wrote the letter to Olive, I had an idea: I'd really pay attention to my visit in the country so I could see what Olive's life was like! Lying around and taking it easy was something I always liked to do. Plus, Aunt Gen was awesome. She was an astronomy professor at a college, so we always got to go to the school's planetarium. The last time we went, I'd convinced my little brother Damien that he was really an alien. That was a good time.

The phone rang, and I heard my mom pick it up. She started laughing almost right away, so I knew it was Aunt Gen. After a little bit, she called out, "MOLLY!"

I slid across the wood floors in the dining room to grab the phone.

"Hey, Aunt Gen!" I yelled into the phone. My mom widened her eyes. She gave me her "use-your-inside-voice" look.

"Hey, honey!" my aunt said. "I'm calling to tell you the planetarium is closed right now. So we'll have to come up with some different things to do. I just didn't want you to be disappointed when you got here."

I was a little disappointed. But I was sure we'd find other things to do. "That's fine," I said.

"Give that brother a hug from me," Aunt Gen said and laughed.

"No way!" I said. Then I yelled, "MOM!" I handed my mom the phone when she walked over.

Not seeing the planetarium was a little sad, but I figured I could just use the time to try to imagine what life was like for Olive. I couldn't wait to hear from her.

After FOUR WHOLE DAYS, I finally got a letter back from Olive. And for the first time in our friendship, she said some things that . . . well, seemed like a challenge.

Dear Molly,

It was great to get your letter. That's so exciting that you get to see your Aunt Gen! I remember you telling me about her. Didn't you tell your brother he was an alien, and he cried so much you had to leave the observatory? Boy, when I write it out like that, it seems kind of mean. But the way you told it was funny.

Anyway, my mom and dad and I laughed pretty hard at your letter. Poughkeepsie is still a city, Molly! It's just a small one. It's not the country . . . It's DEFINITELY not a farm. I don't know how well you'd do on a farm, actually. It's WAY different from a city. There are so many things you have to do all the time. But I do hope you come to visit sometime!

Okay. I should get going. I hope you have fun at Aunt Gen's! Write me and tell me about everything.

BFF. Olive

I stared at the letter and read it one more time. Was Olive really saying I couldn't cut it on a farm?

I paced around my room. Then I sat down at my computer and started an email. Sometimes, four days was WAY TOO LONG to wait for something.

Chapter 2

Olive Takes the Bet

Olive

Molly's letter had made me laugh really hard. Sometimes city people had no idea what it was like on a farm. But then I got an email from Molly and, as usual, she had a great idea.

Dear Olive,

I was so happy to get your letter. But what did you mean about the farm stuff? You know, it's not easy in the city either. You can get lost really easily, or maybe even get hit by a car! You have to know how to get places and how long it will take, and sometimes there are some pretty strange people around.

So I have an idea. Aunt Gen doesn't have a farm, but I bet she knows someone who does! Maybe I could go to a farm for a day and live like you would. And then maybe you could go to a city and live like I would? Then we can see whose life is harder! It'll be a contest. What do you think? We could send each other lists of what we do each day.

I'll win,

Molly

I laughed out loud in my room. I would TOTALLY win this contest.

I ran downstairs and found my mom. "Hey, can we go to Minneapolis soon?" I asked. I'd only been there a couple of times. But

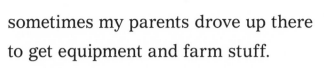

sometimes my parents drove up there to get equipment and farm stuff.

"What's the occasion?" Mom asked. She was sitting on the couch, reading a book.

I showed her the letter. "I want to show Molly that living on a farm takes hard work. And show her how easy it is to live in the city."

Mom looked at me and squinted. She had lived in a city for a lot of years. She chuckled. "You know what, I think this would be good for both of you. We can see if Dad will take you this weekend. We could use some supplies from there, since it's spring and planting season is coming up soon."

I whooped and jumped up and down. "Okay, I need to make a list!" I ran back up to my room, got a notebook and a pen, and ran back down.

I slid into a chair. Then I thought and thought. I tried to come up with things I did most days. But every day was different . . . so I started with what I'd done yesterday.

When I was done, I looked over the list. It was so much!

I felt pretty proud of all we did. Mom and Dad said that even though we didn't make a lot of money, we were rich in work. Which didn't sound great, but really, it was.

I couldn't wait to send off the list to Molly. I thought she might be really impressed with what we did on the farm. And I was 100 percent sure I would win the contest.

Chapter 3

Molly Leaves the City

Molly

I'd sent off my list to Olive. I felt pretty good about the contest! But then I got Olive's list, and I had to admit: I was amazed. She did all of that in one day! It made me wonder why my days felt so busy. So, the next day when we drove to Aunt Gen's, I was NERVOUS. But also determined to make the day at the farm seem like a breeze. I could totally do this.

The drive had taken forever. Like HOURS. And mom had driven us AFTER she'd worked for most of the day, so it already felt super late. The sun was almost all the way set when we pulled into the driveway. Aunt Gen was waiting on the porch of her gigantic old house when we got there. "KITTENS!" she yelled, holding her arms wide.

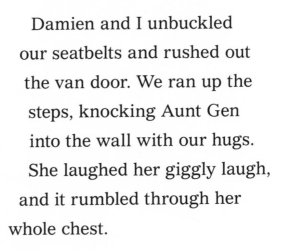

Damien and I unbuckled our seatbelts and rushed out the van door. We ran up the steps, knocking Aunt Gen into the wall with our hugs. She laughed her giggly laugh, and it rumbled through her whole chest.

Mom came up just a few seconds later. "And the big kitten!" Aunt Gen said. Damien and I let go of her, and she and Mom hugged.

"Did you find someone with a farm?" I asked, bouncing on my toes.

Aunt Gen led us inside. "I sure did. We'll talk about it when we get a chance. But first, let's get something to drink and then sit down."

Aunt Gen gave us some soda — my mom lifted her eyebrow about that — and we all sat in the living room. Aunt Gen said, "I knew just the right person to ask for an invitation to a farm. She's eager to meet you, in fact. Agatha has help from her family and some interns, but right now she's a little shorthanded. Plus, she's excited to show a city slicker the farm! She used to live in New York, you know."

My mom stifled a yawn. "Poor thing. Now she's stuck in the country." Aunt Gen pretended to glare at her, and Mom laughed. She stood up, stretched, and looked outside. It was already dark. She grabbed her purse and said, "Okay, little ones, you finish talking about farm things, and I'll get going. Good luck tomorrow, Molly!"

"I don't need luck! This'll be a piece of cake!" I said. Mom looked at Aunt Gen and smiled.

It didn't matter though. I'd show them ALL that a day in the country wouldn't stop me. Olive was the one who had to be worried.

Damien hugged Mom, then I gave her a quick hug, and she left.

I plopped on the couch and yawned big. Aunt Gen looked at me and said, "We need to get you up to bed pretty soon! Farm work comes early, you know."

I didn't really want to go to bed. And I was excited to see Aunt Gen. But, I wanted to win the contest between Olive and me. So I marched right into the bathroom and brushed my teeth. I would find a way to get to sleep. I was in it to win it.

Nothing would stop me from winning this contest.

Minneapolis

26

Olive in the City

Olive

The traffic into Minneapolis was absolutely AWFUL. My dad started grumbling about the bumper-to-bumper cars. "Dang rush hour," he kept saying.

"What's rush hour?" I asked. We were stopped in the middle of the highway. Cars were all I could see in front of and behind us.

"Oh, it's supposedly the times when people are going to or coming from work. But I swear, in Minneapolis, it's rush hour all the time," he said, his hands tightening on the wheel.

Loud music came from a car behind us. Someone next to us had a cigarette dangling out of the car, and I could smell the smoke. Someone else was yelling at someone on the phone.

So far, Minneapolis was just a lot of busy, angry people.

Finally, we started moving again. After about a half hour, we got to downtown Minneapolis. Here we were! I was so excited to be in the city. And DETERMINED that I would win the contest. I mean, the list Molly gave me was so easy. But . . . I had to admit, driving five hours to Minneapolis seemed like forever. And for some reason, it all made my eyes itchy and tired. There was so much to look at! My dad looked tired too.

We drove around in circles to find our hotel and the parking lot. Dad kept talking about "the stupid one-way roads" and kept making our GPS recalculate because he'd miss his street. He could never seem to get in the right lane so we could turn. As I looked out the window, I couldn't believe how many people were on the streets. Some people looked like

they lived on the streets all the time. That made me think a lot.

Finally, we got to the hotel and the parking ramp. We made it to the lobby, and it was huge. I'd never seen so many shiny surfaces. People walked by in suits and in heels. It looked like they would run anyone over who was in front of them.

My dad adjusted his baseball cap and his flannel shirt, then we went to the front desk. "May I help you?" the man at the desk asked.

"Checking in," Dad said. And then I tuned them out. I took in the lobby some more. A huge fountain took up one corner. People sat in chairs and worked on their computers. Most people were on their phones. Outside of the revolving doors, I heard

whistles and saw people dressed in red
uniforms. They would whistle and then
a taxi would come up.

BLAH
BLAH!

Everything was NOISY. Outside horns
honked. Sirens screamed. People talked
and yelled. Inside the rushing sound of
water and the click-clack of shoes on
the floors echoed off the walls.

BLAH
BLAH!

"Okay, noodle, let's go," my dad said.
I put my hands on my backpack straps
and dad shouldered his bag. We walked
across the huge lobby, though it felt like we
were walking across an entire planet. Finally,
we made it to the elevator.

"Eighteenth floor! Isn't that
great?" he said to me and winked.

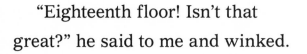

"That's so high!" I said.

My dad laughed. "It sure is. But we'll get to see the whole city from there."

I nodded. We rode up the elevator and got to our floor. When Dad opened the door to our room, I gasped. It was so cool! I'd never been in a hotel as fancy as this one before. Our room had a whole bar area with a coffee pot and bottled water. And a huge TV. We had a small TV in our house, and we hardly ever watched it.

Suddenly I was a little worried. "Dad, did you and Mom have to spend a lot of money to come up here?"

Dad ruffled my hair. "Nope. Your uncle had hotel points he gave to us. This whole thing is free!" He smiled down at me, and I sighed in relief. One thing I knew about farming — you didn't make a lot of money. At least that's what my parents always said. I never really thought about it when I was on the farm. But here in the city, it suddenly felt more important.

 Dad opened the curtains, and I let out a gasp again. "Look at this view!" he said.

The whole city was shining! We were way, way, way far up, and tall buildings stood all around us. It was BEAUTIFUL. We could see the river and lights along it. I saw a boat on the water. We saw all the cars snaking around the roads below us, and even those lights were beautiful. I could still hear the honks and sirens all the way up where we were. But something about it was so exciting!

Looking down the street, I saw theater lights, restaurants, and big billboards . . . All this stuff to do at any time. If you lived in the city, you could just GO to a play or a dance act! Molly had talked about going to art shows and stuff, but I never really understood what she meant. This was what she got to do and see all the time.

"This is so cool!" I said. "But it's REALLY, REALLY LOUD."

My dad chuckled. "It sure is," he said. "There's a reason some people go to the country. But some people like all of this noise and like having all of these things around. You'll get a taste of it more when you're grown up, and then you can decide what you like."

I couldn't imagine a time when I wouldn't want to be on the farm. But I sort of had to admit — the city seemed really fun. And even though all the stuff made me really tired, I still thought I'd win the contest — no problem.

Dad said, "Okay, noodle, your mom has us doing a ton of things tomorrow so it will be like Molly's day. What do you think about staying here in the hotel tonight? We can grab some supper at the restaurant downstairs." I nodded and bounced on my toes. That sounded so great!

At the restaurant, I grabbed the menu on the table. I needed to have a nice, big meal. Because tomorrow I had to show Molly just how easy she had it.

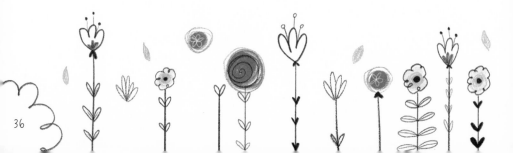

Chapter 5

Molly Meets Stacy

Molly

At 5:00 a.m., I didn't like to talk to people. TOO EARLY. I glared at my aunt. I glared at Damien. I glared at the car we were getting into.

I hadn't slept at all the night before, and now I felt it. Aunt Gen just grinned at me and got into the driver's seat. For some reason, Damien was really peppy.

"Are there tractors there?" he asked my aunt for the millionth time.

"YES," I said and glared.

"Yep," Aunt Gen said. "And there's a plow, and there are goats, and chickens, and cows, and turkeys . . . And I think she might be housing some pigs right now too." Aunt Gen backed out of the driveway, and we set off.

It was still dark out, and as we got out of the city, it got DARK. Like, there were hardly any street lights. Pretty soon, there were none.

"Look up through the window," Aunt Gen said. I did and saw SO MANY STARS. That was so cool. The planetarium was nothing compared to these stars. All the dark, the stars, and the rhythm of the car made me sleepy.

The next thing I knew, we were pulling into a long gravel driveway and pulling up to a big white farmhouse. The sky had lightened a lot, and I could see the sun peeking out over some hills. We must have been driving for a while.

"Well hello! Are these my workers?" a sweet voice said. A wiry woman with twinkling eyes walked over. She wore jeans that were torn, gloves, and huge boots.

Even though it was SO early in the morning, she didn't look tired at all.

Damien popped out of the car. Aunt Gen and I got out too. She and the woman hugged.

"Damien and Molly, this is Agatha," my aunt said. "She is kind enough to show you farm life for the day."

Agatha gave us serious looks. "Oh, they'll have some work to do. Then I don't know if they'll think I'm so nice!" she said with a laugh.

 How hard could it be? I thought. I found my way around a HUGE city every single day. This would be a piece of cake.

 Chickens pecked everywhere. A large rooster strutted around, keeping an eye on us. I heard pigs snort. Over in the pasture lay a giant pig on her side.

Another pig rooted near her. Goats skipped in a pasture way far away. They looked so cute! They made little "baaaa" sounds. Cats slinked up to us and wrapped around our ankles. I bent down to pet them. They meowed and bumped into my hand.

A man and another woman appeared from around the house. They looked like college kids.

"Well," Agatha said, "let's do some introductions, okay? These two are my interns, Scott and Mary Beth. They help around here. Damien, Mary Beth will show you the farm equipment. Scott will do some weeding. And, Molly, you and I are going to start the chores. Does that sound good?"

At that very moment, for the first time ever, I felt shy. I nodded. Aunt Gen put her arm around me and squeezed. "I'm going to hang out in the kitchen for a while and do some housework while you all are out here," she said. "On the farm, everyone works. See you soon. Have fun." She kissed the top of my head and Damien's, and then we all went our separate ways.

I finally found my voice as Agatha and I started walking. "Thank you for letting me come here," I said. My mom told me that no matter what, I needed to thank Agatha.

She smiled at me and said, "Thank YOU. I'm going to get some good work out of you, I can tell. You look strong."

"I am!" I said. "My best friend lives on a farm. She thinks I'm too citified to do chores.

But I walk all the time, and I play soccer and dance . . . This'll be easy." Agatha just smiled at me.

We got to the goat pasture, and I giggled a little. Goats were just goofy looking. Some of them stood and chewed grass. Some of them chased each other. One of them looked at me and baa-ed. I went up to the fence and said, "Can I pet him?"

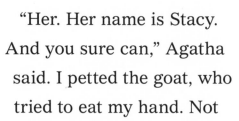

"Her. Her name is Stacy. And you sure can," Agatha said. I petted the goat, who tried to eat my hand. Not in a scary way . . . but still weird and kind of gross. Then out of the corner of my eye, I saw the rooster.

"Hey, did that rooster follow us?" I asked.

Agatha sighed. "Yes. That's Lucian. He's terrible. You'll want to stay away from him. He'll attack you."

Okay, that sounded kind of scary, I thought.

"Let's go milk some goats!" Agatha said. I scrunched my eyebrows and followed her. But I didn't take my eyes off that rooster. The  rooster didn't take his eyes off me either.

And then suddenly, Stacy chomped on my shirt. I pulled, and then she pulled. Then Agatha pulled. It took all our strength to get Stacy to let go of my shirt. Agatha laughed and laughed. "She likes you! Looks like you'll have to keep her!" she said.

I swallowed. If this is what happened when the animals liked you, what happened when they didn't?

Olive Rides the Bus

Olive

I pulled on my sweater and looked out the window at the city.

"So, the first thing your mom says we are to do, is to take the bus to Uptown and then transfer and take another bus to southwest Minneapolis. For breakfast. You up for it?" my dad asked me.

"That's so easy," I said. My eyes felt a lot less tired today. It must have just been that traffic. "Let's do it!"

Dad looked at his phone. "Okay, it says the bus stop is three blocks away, and we just have to wait for 7 minutes. Let's get going!" Dad and I skipped out of the hotel room. I think he was as excited as I was about this trip.

When we got outside, I stopped to look at a sign and someone ran right into me. "Excuse me," the person said. But she said it in a way that sounded like I was the one who should be saying it. Dad and I shared a look.

"Excuse ME," he whispered, and we both giggled.

Dad pointed down the street. "The bus stop is that way!" he said. We started walking, and

I tried to look at everything at once. I also took in the sounds and smells.

A farm is known for bad smells. But the city had ALL KINDS of smells. Some bad smells for sure. But also smells of food baking. Smells of perfume on people walking by. The people were just like the ones in our hotel — well-dressed and busy. And in such a hurry!

We passed by someone playing the saxophone with the case out. "Sometimes people will play music on the street to make money," Dad said.

When I looked in the case, though, I saw only coins. "Can we give him a dollar?" I asked my dad. He nodded, reached in his wallet, got a dollar out, then threw it in the case.

Someone near us eyed Dad's wallet, looking shady. Dad put the wallet in his back pocket. Then he changed his mind and put it in the front pocket in his shirt.

At the intersection, the walk symbol lit up. Dad and I started crossing and then . . . *HOOOONNKKK*. A car — a taxi — almost hit us! It got so close to us, Dad could have laid on the hood. The cab driver yelled at us for being in the way.

My dad, who never yells at anyone, yelled back, "You could have killed us!" Then he pointed to the walk sign. This didn't make the driver any less angry.

We hurried across the street with my heart beating out of my chest! Did Molly deal with this every day? Angry people? Almost getting hit by cars? Worrying about someone stealing your wallet? The thoughts made my brain tired.

And we hadn't even gone anywhere yet. Maybe city life was harder than I thought . . . But still. Not as hard as living on a farm. I would still win this contest. I breathed in deeply to get my heart to slow down.

Finally, we got to the bus stop. Both Dad and I were frazzled. He kept adjusting his baseball cap and saying, "It's a crazy place."

We stood by the bus stop sign and Dad pointed up. "This tells us what buses stop here," he said. "We're taking the number 21 . . ." He trailed off, then closed his eyes.

"What's wrong?" I asked.

"We went the wrong way. This isn't our stop," he said.

So far, things in the city had NOT been very easy.

We looked at each other and both burst out laughing. Then we walked all the way back to the hotel, then all the way to the bus stop we should have gone to in the first place.

This time, though, I knew that if the light said to go, we should double check to make sure no one was turning right into us. And this time, my dad didn't take out his wallet. We also avoided the fast-moving people on the sidewalk.

We got to the RIGHT bus stop, and the bus pulled up. Dad let me put the money in the machine, and we got on. As we started to walk down the aisle, the bus lurched forward. Dad and I had to grab onto the poles. I almost fell into someone's lap! Luckily, she gave me a sweet smile and said, "That happens to me every time."

The bus was so crowded, we couldn't sit down. That was fine because I could look out the windows and see lots of things. We drove by countless stores — way more than in Sioux City. And people. People everywhere. People, cars, buses . . . People walked their dogs, huddled and talked, walked in and out of stores. It seemed like so much fun. But so BUSY. I already felt like we'd been through a whole day. But we hadn't even had breakfast! I saw more people in an hour than I did in three days in Iowa. And more people who all looked so different.

I loved that part — seeing all the different types of people. But I was already so hungry. And really frustrated. There was too much to pay attention to all the time here.

We made it to our stop, and Dad let me pull the cord for the "request stop." I smiled, and lots of people on the bus smiled back. We got out, and Dad checked the schedule.

"Okay, we just have to wait . . . 15 minutes for our bus," he said. We waited, and it seemed like FOREVER. Finally, our second bus came. This time, we found seats, but people didn't seem as nice. After 20 more minutes, we got to our second stop.

By now, it was already 8:30. We'd left our hotel at 7:30. Not only was I really frustrated and annoyed, I was also SUPER hungry.

"How far away is the restaurant?" I asked.

Dad said, "Just a couple of blocks." We walked to the restaurant, and I was surprised

that my feet were starting to hurt. On the farm, I ran around all the time. So that was weird. I was really looking forward to sitting down and eating.

The restaurant was called "Hot Plate" and looked a little fancy. But I didn't care — I just wanted food! Dad went up to the hostess and said, "Two, please."

She looked down and said, "Okay, that'll be a 45-minute wait."

Dad and I looked at each other with huge, wide eyes.

Molly Gets a Goat

Molly

Stacy would not leave me alone. She HAD BEEN cute. Now, she was just annoying. I couldn't get rid of her. She was as bad as Damien! "Let go of my shirt!" I yelled, for the millionth time.

I stood knee deep in straw that scratched at my legs. I felt straw in my sleeves and up my pants legs. Straw everywhere. Then, Stacy butted her head into my back, and I tripped forward, landing on my chest. I blew out straw from my mouth. Because I was sweaty,

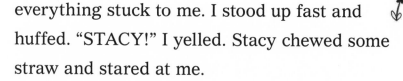

everything stuck to me. I stood up fast and huffed. "STACY!" I yelled. Stacy chewed some straw and stared at me.

The SMELL of the barn was the worst. I didn't realize that "mucking out" something meant cleaning up . . . POOP. Smelly, icky, gross poop. Not a lot — the goats mostly went outside — but enough!

Plus, my hands hurt from using the pitchfork to change out the hay. And I'd been working for only an hour! I couldn't believe Olive did this all the time.

Then it was time to feed the chickens. I put down the pitchfork and was about to leave, when Stacy grabbed my shirt again!

"STACY!" I yelled, grabbing the end of my shirt. Stacy grabbed harder. So I pulled harder.

"Let. Go. Of. My. SHIRT!" I yelled, pulling and pulling. No way would I let that goat win. She had grabbed my shirt TOO MANY TIMES. I pulled extra, extra hard.

RIIIIPPPPPP!

The bottom part of my shirt ripped off, and this time I staggered backward. I staggered backward right into . . .

POOP.

SPLAT! My boot stepped right in it, and then I slipped and fell on my rear end. Luckily, it was not on the poop. But I was ankle deep in it on my right foot! It covered the rain boot that Aunt Gen made me wear.

I was so grateful for boots right then! But wow did I smell.

I looked over at Stacy and narrowed my eyes. Now she chewed on my shirt and looked at me.

"That wasn't nice, Stacy!" I said to her as I stood up.

Stacy swallowed and said, "Baaaa."

I huffed out again and left the pen, trying to rub the poo off anything I came up against. I saw a fence, so I rubbed part of my boot off. Then I used grass. Finally, most of it was off, and I started to make my way to the chicken coop. Stacy followed along the fence. Thank goodness she couldn't get out!

As I trudged toward the chicken coop, something flashed in the corner of my eye. It couldn't have been Stacy. I checked, and Stacy stood right at the fence, staring at me. I glared at her and started walking again.

Something flashed again! When I looked this time, I finally saw what it was. It was the rooster, Lucian. But he looked like he was just pecking along on the ground, not paying any attention to me.

So I kept walking, keeping Lucian in my side vision. He started walking right when I did. I stopped. Lucian stopped and started pecking at the ground again.

I walked two steps and stopped suddenly.
Lucian walked two steps and stopped suddenly.

The rooster was following me.

I could see Agatha and the
chicken coop up ahead, not
too far. I looked at Lucian.
He looked at me.

AND I RAN!

I ran as fast as I
could to Agatha, yelling,
"ROOSTER ROOSTER
ROOSTER!"

Agatha looked up and saw
me running. Then her face darkened.
I could tell Lucian was right behind me.
Luckily, I'm REALLY fast, so I made it to

Agatha just in time. Lucian flew just a little bit in the air, with his feet and spurs out.

Agatha used her foot to nudge him back by his chest. He floated backward in the air! He came at Agatha again, and she nudged him harder, so he floated back harder.

"Lucian," she said. "Do you want to become someone's chicken dinner?" This somehow seemed to stop him. He waddled away, like nothing had happened.

Agatha looked at him fondly. "He's such a crazy bird," she said. "But I love him. We do this about once a week."

My eyes got wide. "Once a week?" I asked.

She nodded. "It's his job to take care of the hens," she explained. "He takes it very

seriously. He's just looking out for them.
And we have a nice relationship now.
I think he's probably just on high alert
because of new people."

"Would he really have attacked me?"
I asked.

Agatha looked serious. "Yes," she said.
"Just keep your eye out for him." She put
her nose in the air and sniffed. "Honey, did
you . . . sit in poo?"

I sighed and pointed to my still-dirty
boot. "I stepped in it."

She patted my shoulder. "You get used to
it," she said with a laugh. "Oh, hey. There's
Stacy. How did she get out?"

I turned around with my eyes wide. Stacy
stood just a few feet back, looking at me. She
baa-ed, then trotted over to me. She butted into
me, and I stumbled forward.

Agatha laughed and laughed. "Looks like
you made a friend for life," she said.

Stacy grabbed my sleeve and started to pull.
I sighed.

Chapter 8

Olive Gets Lost

Olive

Breakfast was SO GOOD, even if it took us forever to sit down and eat. Once we finished, we had to figure out how to take the bus to a community center and then to the streets to shop.

That sounded easy, but after our morning, I was starting to think it WASN'T so easy. Just to go have breakfast took us two hours!

On the bus, one person sat in the back and talked on the phone loudly. One person sang along to her headphones. One person was asleep in one of the seats.

The bus dropped us off at our stop, and we walked to the community rec center. That HAD been easy. Dad and I looked at each other and high-fived.

"Is that really it? We just had to take the bus to the community center?" I asked.

Dad shrugged. "I think we're making the day happen like Molly's day is," he said. "So, she'd probably go here for a class or something. But now our schedule says . . . go to Uptown again. It looks like we can take the metro line. We get to take a train!"

I clapped my hands. I knew that Molly took the train every day — this was a lot like that.

"How far away is it?" I asked.

Dad's shoulders slumped. "It's about a mile — a 20-minute walk," he said. "Or, we could wait for the next bus, which comes in 45 minutes."

My feet hurt A LOT. But waiting for the bus sounded awful.

"I guess we should walk," I said. Dad nodded, but I could tell he didn't like it either. We dragged ourselves down the street and walked for 20 minutes to the train station. Dad went to the ticket kiosk.

He stared at it.

I stared at it.

I had no idea what it meant. Dad mumbled all the directions out loud: "Press this button if you want a day pass . . . or this button if you want a week pass . . . or a monthly pass . . . for a card go to metrotransit.com . . . to upload more money, press your card to the . . ." There didn't seem to be a button for just buying a ticket!

Looking around, I didn't see anyone to give our tickets to. "Dad, how do we get on the train? There's no one to give a ticket to." He had figured out which tickets to buy and was getting money out.

"I don't — I'm not sure," he said. "Let me get these tickets, and then I'll look it up on my phone."

The tickets came out, but before he could look it up, our train came! It whooshed into the station, and the wind blew back my hair.

Dad said, "Let's get on the train, and I'll read about it."

I didn't like that. It felt like we were stealing. But we got on the train, and it whooshed us away.

I loved the train — well, mostly. I was so worried that someone would come and yell at us or kick us off. So it was hard to even look at the great scenery. Finally, we reached our stop and got off.

"Now where to?" I asked.

Dad closed his eyes and groaned. "The bus," he said.

"UGHHH," I said, and slumped into Dad.

After a million transfers and a million smells, Dad and I made it to Uptown. Our jobs were to get my hair cut, to look at an art gallery, and to grab some pet food. AND fit lunch in there somewhere. The streets of Uptown were just as crowded as they were downtown. Here, people wore weird clothes and had really big beards. They weren't all business-y the way the downtown people were. Lots of these people had different colored hair and lots of tattoos. They looked like really cool, but kind of scary, college kids.

Dad and I found the hair place, and I went in. The girl at the front desk had a huge pink Mohawk.

"Do you have an appointment?" she asked.

I nodded. "I'm Olive," I squeaked.

"Oh, yes!" the girl said. "We got a call from your mom, and she set up your appointment. She told us to give you a pink Mohawk like I have."

My eyes got huge. I looked at my dad and opened my mouth. Then the girl smiled. "I'm just kidding!" she said. "But I think you should

do something fun today." Then she looked at my dad and said, "We could do your hair, too, you know."

Dad laughed. "No, no, this is Olive's day," he said.

The girl led me to a chair. "Jasmine will be your stylist," she said.

A woman in super high heels rushed out. "You must be Olive!" she said. "I know just the thing for you." And for the next hour, she talked my ears off as she cut my hair.

She'd also talked me into a purple streak. When it was time for me to look in the mirror, I was nervous. She turned the chair around, and my mouth dropped open: It barely even looked like me! She had done something really big and really weird to my

hair. And though I loved the purple streak, it was hardly noticeable because of my hairstyle.

"Don't you love it?" Jasmine squealed.

"Uh. . . ," I said.

She led me to the cash register where my dad was. His eyes got huge. "Well . . ." was all he said.

And I agreed.

When we walked out, Dad said, "So, you're probably going to want to wash out your hair pretty soon, right?"

I nodded.

Dad saw the pet food store and the art gallery. They were side-by-side. "I know this is cheating just a little," he said, "but why don't you go to the art gallery, and I'll go to the pet store. Then we'll meet back here in 10 minutes."

That was a great idea. It meant we got to go back to the hotel earlier! I said yes, and then we split up.

The art gallery was so neat. HUGE, GINORMOUS drawings took up the entire wall. The drawings had tiny people etched into them. Some of them had whole scenes, but some were really small. I loved it. I was the only one in the place, except the owner.

He didn't trust me — he kept circling around me like a rooster. I totally lost track of time looking at the art. I realized I'd been in there for more than 15 minutes and raced out.

Dad wasn't there. But there was a mime standing on the corner.

I went into the pet store and looked all around. Dad wasn't anywhere! I started to feel a little panicky. The mime on the corner might have seen something, so I walked up to him.

"Excuse me, sir," I said.

The mime looked at me and opened his eyes wide. He nodded. I guessed that was him answering me?

"Um, have you seen a guy in a red shirt and a red baseball hat?" I asked. "And jeans? And John Deere boots?"

The mime put his finger to his chin and looked out across the street thoughtfully. Then his face brightened, and he nodded. He pointed to the park across the street and then mimed walking.

"You saw him walk across the street?" I asked.

He nodded. Then he mimed a hat blowing off of his head. He looked around with big eyes. Then he pointed across the street to the park. Then he pretended he was chasing after something.

I totally got it!

"My dad's hat blew off, so he chased it across the street to the park?" I asked.

The mime nodded super fast.

"You're a really good mime!" I said.

The mime grinned and then pretended to give me a high five.

Just as I was about to sprint across the street, I saw my dad jogging toward me. He caught up to me and put his arm around my shoulder. "Boy, there's always something going on here," he said. "Sorry if I scared you, honey! I don't know about you, but I'm ready to go home. Should we go?"

"YES, please," I said.

Before we turned away, the mime gave us the thumbs up sign.

Chapter 9

Molly Goes Home

Molly

It seemed like the day had lasted forever, but FINALLY, it was over. By the time we all piled into the car, I was covered in poo and dirt. I had blisters on my hands. My shirt was torn in about six places. And Stacy stared at me from outside the car and chewed on grass happily. I glared at her.

I was so tired I could barely keep my eyes open. Damien, somehow, was still all cheery! He couldn't stop talking about the tractor and the plow and the pigs. It was like we had two different days. Maybe he really was an alien.

I had to admit: Olive was one tough farm girl. She was right! I couldn't cut it living on a farm.

She had definitely won this contest.

When we got back to the house, I took a long shower. Then I asked Aunt Gen if I could get on her computer to IM with Olive. I got on Skype and right away saw Olive's handle. I took a deep breath.

I had to come clean. I started writing.

Oh my gosh, Olive. I'm SO TIRED. You were right — farming is crazy hard work. I hate to admit it, but . . . I think you won the contest.

Hi, Molly! Well, I'm not sure about that. I need to say sorry to you! I thought your schedule was so easy. IT ISN'T. We got lost so many times. And it took a long time to get places. And my hair looks really weird. I think YOU might have won the contest.

 Your hair looks weird?!

Yeah, but I think my mom was playing a joke on me. Anyway . . . both my dad and me are so tired tonight. I thought I was in good shape because of the farm, but my feet hurt! You walk so much!

 My whole body hurts! And I slipped in poo. And a goat ate my shirt.

I went into everything that had happened to me that day. Olive explained her day to me too. We laughed — a lot.

One thing we both agreed on: It was hard in both places. Maybe we'd BOTH won the contest.

I'm really glad I got to see a little bit what your life might be like.

Yeah, same with me about your life. But one other thing? I really like where I live.

And at the exact same time, Olive wrote, *I will be staying on the farm.* I laughed when I saw that, and I imagined her laughing all the way in Iowa.

Best friends forever?

Best friends forever.

After we got off of IM, Aunt Gen came over and rubbed my shoulders. "A little harder than you thought, huh?"

I nodded, my eyes wide. "I always thought the country was —"

Aunt Gen jumped in, "Simple?"

"Yes!" I said. "But there were so many things we had to remember and do. It wasn't just hard work — it took a lot of thinking."

Aunt Gen handed me a soda. "That it does. Are you happy to go back to New York?" she asked.

I sipped the soda happily. "Oh, yes," I said. "I don't think farm life is for me!"

"Well, I know at least one kid who will be disappointed with that," Aunt Gen said.

"Olive?" I asked. Though I thought Olive would understand.

"Oh, no," Aunt Gen said, grinning. "Your new best friend, Stacy." She ruffled my hair, and I groaned.

If I never petted another goat again, I would be just fine.

About the Author

Megan Atwood lives and works in Minneapolis, Minnesota. She has written more than 35 children's books and teaches creative writing at Hamline University. When she is not writing books or teaching, she is inflicting love and affection on her cats and dreaming up more characters to keep her company. She also is trying to find more time to write personal letters to her loved ones, much like Molly and Olive.

Megan Atwood

About the Illustrator

Originally from London, Gareth now lives in beautiful Somerset with his wife and two boys. He works from his home studio alongside his ever-faithful assistant, Herbie the Jack Russell. After studying illustration at Bournemouth College of Art and Design and working in-house for the majority of his career, Gareth took the plunge to go freelance seven years ago and hasn't looked back.

Gareth Llewhellin

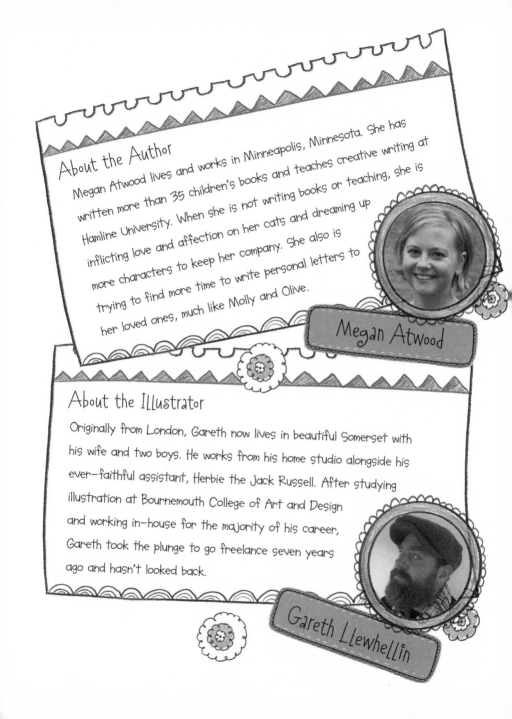

Glossary

contest—a game that people try to win

grateful—thankful

IM—instant message

instant—happening right away

mime—a performer who doesn't speak

Mohawk—a hairstyle in which the head is shaved, except for a strip of hair along the middle

nervous—tense or fearful

pasture—land where farm animals eat and exercise

planetarium—a building or room that has special equipment for projecting pictures of the stars, planets, and other space objects and their movements onto a rounded ceiling, or dome

saxophone—a musical instrument made of brass

seriously—not lightly

stagger—to walk unsteadily

trudge—to walk slowly and with effort

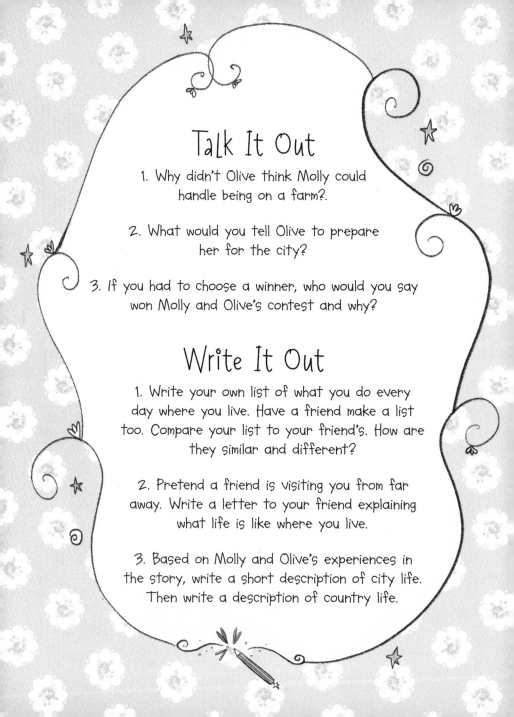

Talk It Out

1. Why didn't Olive think Molly could handle being on a farm?.

2. What would you tell Olive to prepare her for the city?

3. If you had to choose a winner, who would you say won Molly and Olive's contest and why?

Write It Out

1. Write your own list of what you do every day where you live. Have a friend make a list too. Compare your list to your friend's. How are they similar and different?

2. Pretend a friend is visiting you from far away. Write a letter to your friend explaining what life is like where you live.

3. Based on Molly and Olive's experiences in the story, write a short description of city life. Then write a description of country life.

A Letter for You!

Dear friend,

It's Molly. Oh my gosh, I found out that farm work is SO HARD. But, I have to admit — it's really fun. My favorite part was the animals. Even if that goat was a pain.

When I got home, I looked up some cool animal facts:

★ Pigs don't sweat, so they roll in the mud to stay cool!

★ Did you know cows have best friends in their herds? (I can understand that — best friends are the BEST.)

★ Some goats like to climb trees.

★ Chickens talk to each other! They have 24 sounds they use to tell each other about food, and danger, and stuff.

I hope you liked these facts! Can you look up any more? There are so many other cool animals out there.

Okay, I have to go tell Olive what I learned! She probably knows all of this,. but maybe I can surprise her anyway!

Cock-a-doodle-doo!!!

Molly

The fun doesn't stop here!

Discover more at www.capstonekids.com

Videos & Contests

Games & Puzzles

Friends & Favorites

Authors & Illustrators

Find cool websites and more books like this one
at www.facthound.com. Just type in the Book ID:
9781515829218 and you're ready to go!